This Book Belongs To

....

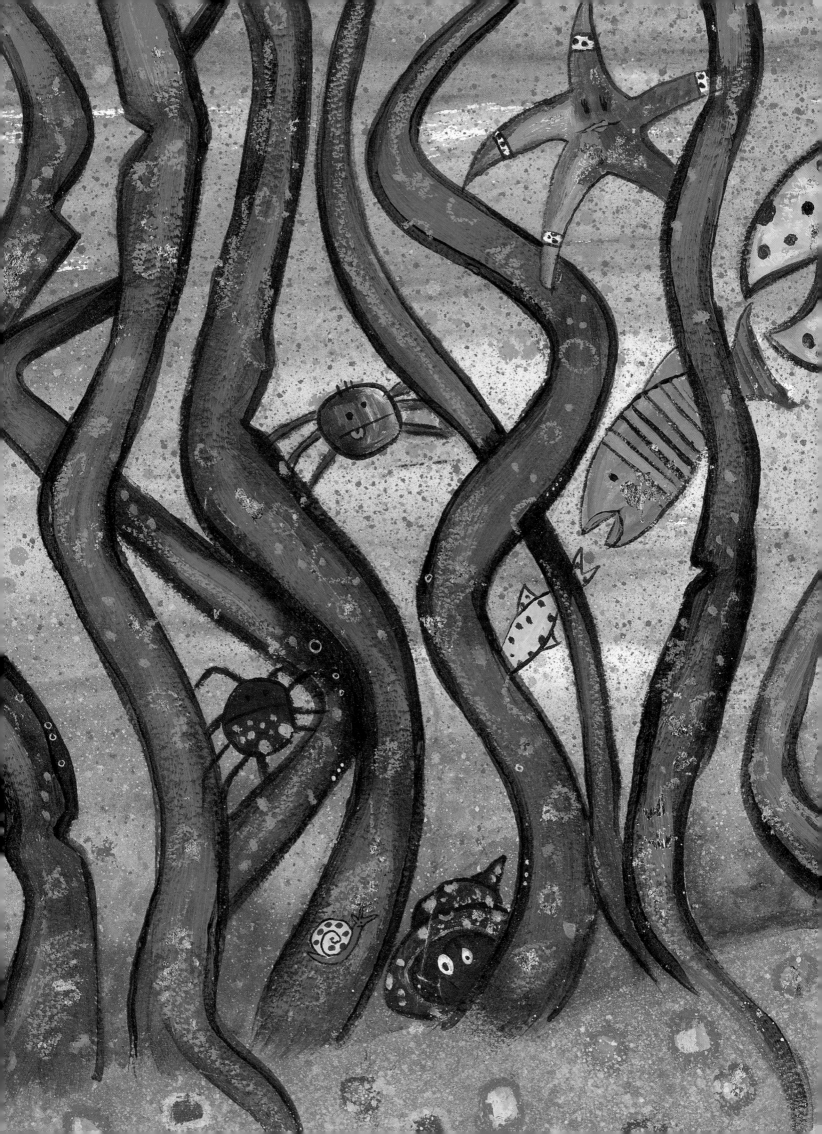

For my husband Tim, my boys Hugh, William and Henry,
and my mum and dad Vi and Pete - JH

For Laura and my family - RC

Published by
Starlet Limited

FIRST EDITION
ISBN 0-9551098-1-7
ISBN 978-0-9551098-1-2

Text and Illustrations
Copyright © 2005 Starlet Limited

PRINTED IN THE UNITED KINGDOM

Michelle

in

Crabbit Comes to Stay

By Julie Hegarty

Illustrated by Ritchie Collins

Down by the ocean; deep, dark and cool,
Lives a shell called Michelle in a magic rock pool

One day in her home
That she cleans and looks after,
She heard crying and sobbing;
Not fun and laughter.

Peeping over her rock,
She looked down and saw
Her little friend Hermie
with his head in his claw.

"Oh dear," she said as she heard him groaning,
"Whatever's wrong, Hermie? Why are you moaning?
You look so worried and sound so sad.
What can it be that makes you feel bad?"

"Oh, Michelle, it's just terrible;
Worst day of the year.
It's this letter," said Hermie,
Wiping a tear,
"From my cousin Crabbit,
Who's coming to stay.
He's so rude and grumpy
And nasty all day."

Poor Hermie was shaking, "I'll explain more fully:
When we were both little, he was a big bully."

Oh, is that all?" asked Michelle with a smile.
All!" Hermie cried. "But Crabbit's so vile!"
I'm sure he'll have changed from a young crustacean
And grown out of it now," was Michelle's explanation.

Hermie, still anxious, said, "Maybe you're right,
But I'm not so sure. He still gives me a fright.

Can I read you this letter
So you can hear what he wrote?
It's written how he talks.
It reads, and I quote:
'I'm coming on Friday
At around twelve o'clock.
Make sure lunch is ready
And you've tidied your rock.

"I'm Coming on Friday
at around twelve o'clock.
Make sure lunch is ready
and you've tidied your rock.
I want all your toys
put neatly away.
Better look after me
And be free
that day!

I want all your toys
Put neatly away,
Better look after me
And be free that day!'"
"My goodness!" said Michelle.
"He's bossy and rude.
Fancy expecting all that:
Hide your toys! Eat your food!"

"Hermie! Where are you? It's Crabbit, it's me.
Come fetch my case and make me some tea."
"I told you," said Hermie. "Oh, what will I do?"
"Jump up here," said Michelle. "I'll look after you."

At Crabbit's bellowing,
Hermie shivered and shook.

LEITH

NEW YORK

FIFE

PARIS

"Be calm," said Michelle.
"Let's take a look."
"Don't think I can't see you.
Come now!" Crabbit scolded.
And he stared up at them
As he stood with claws folded.

"Hello, Cousin Crabbit," poor Hermie stuttered.
"Get out of that pool," his big cousin muttered.

Hermie did as he was told
And approached Crabbit meekly.
"Oh, you haven't changed a bit.
Still pathetic and weakly.

Show me your muscles. Here, look at mine!"
Crabbit raised up his pincers in the bright sunshine.

Michelle was quite scared
(Crabbit being bad mannered),
But bravely marched over.
"Please stop it," she stammered.

"Who's this little thing?" Crabbit laughed out loudly.
"I'm Hermie's best friend," she answered him proudl
"And not only that, he has other friends too.
He's popular round here and not a bit like you!"

"Oooh!" mocked Crabbit,
With a sneer on his face,
"Are you in his gang
Who hang round this place?"

"That's right," said Michelle,
"And you can play if you want.
But you have to be friendly,
Or otherwise you can't!"

Then along came Starfish, taking them by surprise.
And as usual, Starfish wanted her exercise.
"Star jumps everybody," she said. "Bend and reach.
Then line up behind me for a swim at the beach."

Michelle turned to Crabbit,
But now couldn't see him.
"Where are you?" she called.
"It's time for a swim."
They all looked around,
And from deep in his shell,
Crabbit spat, "Leave me alone!
I don't feel very well."

"Come swimming," said Starfish. "You know what to do
"I can't! And I won't! Go away! Boo-hoo!"
"What is it?" asked Hermie, sidling up to him.
"You're a crab," he said. "All crabs can swim."

"All except me," Crabbit sobbed as he told
Of when he was young and naughty and bold.
"I just didn't listen to what Mummy said,
And now I can't swim and get teased instead."

"So that's why you bully and treat Hermie so badly. It's because you were bullied," Michelle added sadly. "I forgive you," said Hermie. "We'll teach you to swim Come with us now." And they all jumped in.

By the end of the day, Crabbit swam round the pool.
"I'm the happiest crab. Hermie you're cool.
Now I can go home with my head held high,
And when the crabs swim, I won't hide and cry."

"Hooray!" They both cheered,

Throwing their claws in the sk

And now, when Crabbit visits, he's as nice as pie.

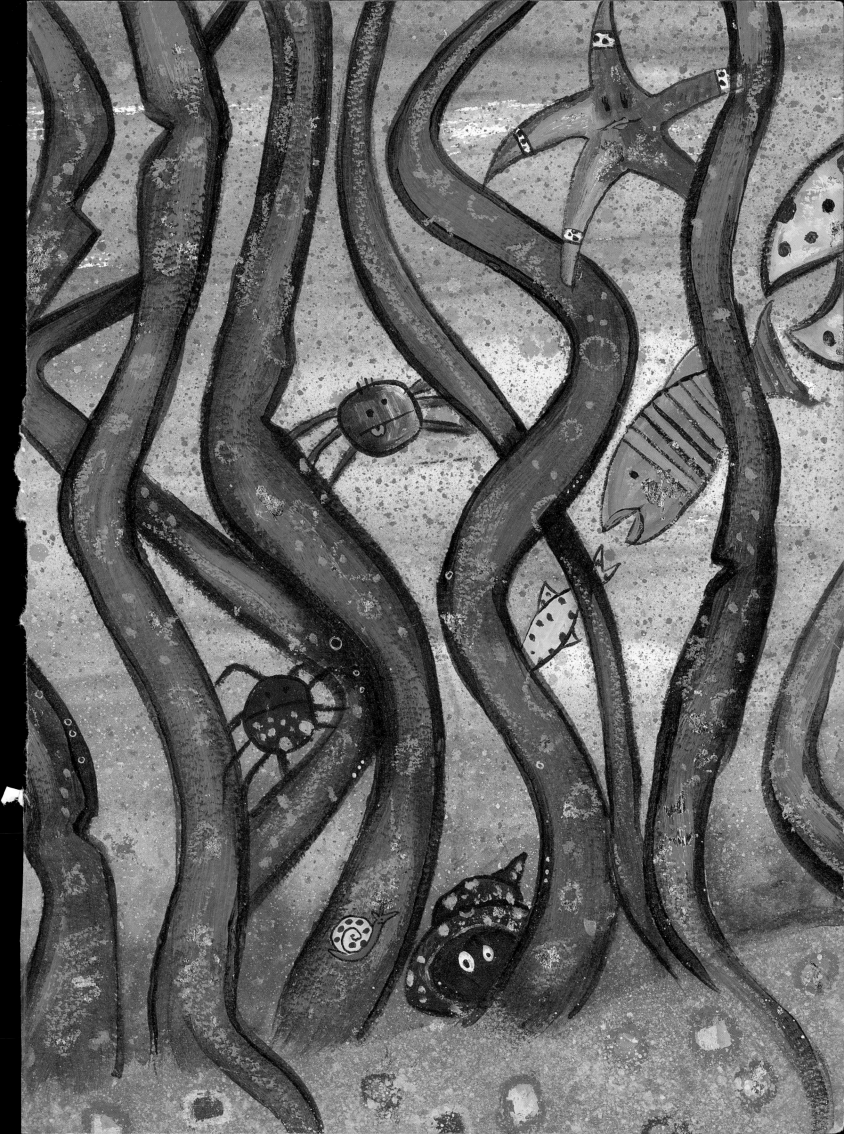

Michelle, Hermie and Crabbit

would like you to know that full book size prints of the pictures in this story-book are available online at **www.juliehegarty.com**

They are all beautifully printed on artist's paper and are signed by the artist Ritchie Collins.

Starfish says "Why not collect a set?"